Misfit Toys

Josh K. Stevens

To A.H., D.H., K.N, K.M., C.D., D.P., C.B., E.L., and B.Z.
The real-life Misfit Toys, the inspiration for this story,
and some of the greatest people ever.
Thank you for listening to me on all those crazy nights that served
as never ending fodder for the stories in my head.
I can not express how much that meant to me.

Misfit Toys

Ode to the Misfit Toys

Prologue
    A chance encounter
A dark night
Strangers become friends
People grow together
The curtain rises
Enter the room
Set down my jacket and stand
Faceless shadows sit around motionless
Non-existent eyes never blinking
Pass me a beer
Echoes off the walls
Already in my hand
The beer is getting warm and perspiring
No one moves
No one said anything at all
The dim light flickers
Shadows cover it up
Swarming writhing shadows
They are alive and moving
Taking my soul as they move

Locusts move through my universe,
Devouring everything in their wake.
Buzzing wings are all I hear
Followed by shrieks of torment
Smoke is all I see
Fire bursts forth and ignites everything
As they tear down the brimstone street
Riding in like horsemen.
Four to be exact.
And they brought with them
Among other visitors
And various suffering
Pestilence, Famine
War, Death
The final one came none too soon
And with far too much pain
Silence
From this outcrop
I recall
There was sun light once
Not too long ago
I felt it on my face
I swam through it
Comfortable
At home
At peace
Like an infant in the womb
It felt grand

The calliope rang out
Deafening happiness
I wore a top hat
The circus played around me
Three rings and a big top
Clowns and animals
Popcorn and peanuts
Good times had by all
It packed up and left town
Tore down the big top
Shot the clowns and animals
Poisoned the popcorn and peanuts
Plucked the sun from the sky
Popped it between giant fingers like a grape
I never should've been here in the first place
Only gray inklings now
Sun pokes through now and again
I race to catch it
I'm not as fast as I once was
Never able to reach it
It doesn't even graze my fingertips
Like it once did
Dark clouds loom overhead
Yesterday they were on the horizon
Almost out of sight
They turned around and jumped back
To stand above me
Sound like a sheet being torn in two

Water bursts forth from the billowing sails
It looks like blood
I step off the edge
I'm falling faster than the rain now
It's going to catch up with me soon
The ground meets my flesh
The water meets my back
Gray matter fills the world
The organ takes up where the calliope left off
The tattered curtain falls
Epilogue
Evaporation takes place
Existence turns to vapor
Memory turns to smoke
The wind picks up
I just fade away.

The Body in the Bathroom

Considering the fact that there was a dead body in the bathroom, everyone in the room was relatively relaxed.

Maybe relaxed wasn't the right word.

For the first time anyone could remember, everyone in the room was quiet, sitting motionless on the ragtag furniture scattered about the studio apartment. For some groups of friends, this probably wouldn't have seemed very out of the ordinary but, for the Misfit Toys, this was highly unusual, compared to the usual chaotic carnival of laughter, shouting, and music that was par for the course every night they were together. While no one was quite sure what to say or what to do, as of yet, no one was freaking out and, in Josh's opinion, that was a major league upside.

The door to the bathroom was closed now, and the six friends were strewn about the living area of the studio apartment, most of their eyes trained on the floor, allowing the realization of what had just happened swim slowly through the drunkenness that had previously been clouding their minds. You could feel the heaviness in the air and, in this case, it wasn't the cigarette smoke weighing down everyone's shoulders.

Everyone was thinking of the problem, but no one could seem to come up with a solution.

Josh stood from his sitting position on the futon and lit a cigarette as he paced back and forth along the wall, running his hand through his hair. He took a deep drag off the smoke and ashed into an empty beer can that was sitting on top of the television.

"Okay. Let's run through this again," Josh said, shattering the morbid serenity, causing the group, who had grown accustomed to the weighted silence, jumped as a collective entity. Josh, staring out the window, didn't even seem to notice, "What the hell is going on?"

"You have a dead body in your bathroom," Dan replied, as if, by pointing out the obvious fact, he was going to help at this particular juncture. Kathleen shot him a look from her spot on the couch. Dan raised his eyebrows and shrugged the glare off. He muttered under his breath, "Well, he does."

"Seriously, what would compel you to knife a guy in my bathroom?" Josh asked, glaring at Andy. Andy opened his mouth to plead his case but, before he even had a chance to formulate a response, Dan jumped in.

"Josh, let's be serious, we were all thinking about it," he said, "Andy just beat us to the punch."

Josh pointed at Dan, trying to come up with a crushing retort, but he could think of nothing. He raised his eyebrows, considering the fact and, realizing that what Dan had said not only made sense, but was, in fact, the truth, he dropped his hand to his side. Aside from Kristen, no one in the room enjoyed Dave's company. It was hard to say whether or not they enjoyed his company more or less now that he was a newly fresh corpse laying askew in the bathtub. Dave was, in short, ignorant and obnoxious and he had punctuated each of his terribly unfunny jokes with racial slurs. This evening they had been primarily focused on the Asian community. A fact that did not please Andy, whose forebears hailed from the Philippines.

"A better question would be what the hell are we going to do about this?" Kathleen asked, "Because, as of right now, we're all going to go to jail."

"You guys won't go to jail," Andy piped up from his spot beside Dan, "I'm the one who did it. You guys are just bystanders. I'm gonna end up in the clink."

"Fuck that," Josh said, "No one is going to jail. While Kathleen's question is a good one that deserved asking, there's a better and more important question that we should be discussing."

Everyone stared at Josh, waiting for him to finish his thought. He calmly took another drag off of his cigarette as he made his way across the room and snuffed out the butt in the ashtray on his kitchen counter. He walked back across the room and leaned against the television stand, looking at each member of the group and letting the tension build. Josh loved being the center of attention and it showed. He let his eyes slowly travel from left right across the room. Kathleen, Kristen, Andy, Dan. Just as the anticipation was about to become unbearable, Dan gasped and jumped to his feet.

"What do we do with the body?" Dan asked, overly excited. Josh pointed at him with a nod. Dan pumped his fists victoriously in the air then sank back to his spot on the futon.

"We can't just dispose of the body," Kathleen said, "We have to..." She trailed off, not really knowing what else to say. Her eyes fell on Andy. Andy raised his eyebrows. Kathleen's eyes shifted to Kristen. Kristen had been abnormally quiet considering that she was usually the most talkative of the bunch. Everyone else talked a lot, particularly if they had things to say, whereas Kristen spoke constantly, even if she had absolutely nothing to say. She was especially vocal if there was an issue that needed to be solved, no matter how inexperienced she may have been on the subject at hand. One would have assumed that a situation like the one that they were dealing with at the present time would've been Kristen's time to shine. Unfortunately, it had been Kristen who had invited Dave to the apartment in the first place. Kathleen moved across the couch and placed an arm over her shoulder.

"Kristen? What do you think about this?" Kathleen asked.

"Nope. Sorry. She doesn't get a vote. She's in no state of mind to comment on this thing," Josh said, exhaling the smoke from his lungs as his voice raised in pitch and speed, "Besides, this whole mess is her fault."

"It was her boyfriend," She snarled, glaring at Josh.

"He wasn't my boyfriend, we were 'seeing each other'," Kristen said, cutting off any further arguments from taking place. Kathleen jumped backwards, taken off guard by Kristen's sudden vocalization. Kristen shook her head, blinking her eyes, and looked around the room, "And I say, we should get rid of this problem on our own. There'll be too many questions asked by the cops."

"Well, she's obviously in a better state of mind than I thought," Josh stated, "That's two votes for taking care of this in house. Anyone else?"

"That's fucking ridiculous," Kathleen said, shaking her head as she leaned against the back of the couch and crossed her arms over her chest, "What about Dave?"

"What about Dave? He had it coming," Kristen said, "I thought this was already established."

"A much, much better state of mind than I thought," Josh said with a nod. He lit up another cigarette and the room fell silent. Josh looked around the room slowly, "So, the question remains, who's on board?"

"I am most definitely in," Dan said. Andy and Kristen both nodded their agreement. All eyes fell on Kathleen, whose only response was the grinding sound of her teeth clenching.

"Well?" Josh asked, cocking an eyebrow giving a slight shrug of his shoulders. Kathleen stood up and made her way to the kitchen without a word, though her stomping feet seemed to be answer enough. She began rifling through the lackluster contents of Josh's kitchen cabinets, not bothering to close them behind her. After a moment of searching, she found what she was looking for. From the cabinet above the sink, she produced a water glass and slammed it on the counter. Her eyes met Josh's and, without breaking eye contact, she tore the cap off of the no-name vodka bottle on the counter, upended it, and filled the glass halfway. Slamming the bottle back down, she raised the glass in the air, muttering something under her breath that sounded more like a profanity laced prayer than a toast. She closed her eyes and, after a slow exhalation, she brought the glass to her lips and poured the liquid in her mouth, not stopping until the glass was empty. She made no outward reaction the liquor, merely lowering her head and standing in silence for another few seconds. After another extended exhalation, she looked up and slowly gave a single nod of her head.

"I guess I'm in," she said, taking a cigarette from her pack and lighting it.

"Okay," Josh said with a sigh of relief. He clapped his hands together, "Then, it's unanimous. Andy, we're going to keep you out of the big house." Andy smiled and gave a thumbs up, which Josh proudly returned.

"Provided, that we don't fuck the disposal process up," Kathleen muttered. She poured another glass of vodka. Josh lowered his head, closed his eyes, and began rubbing his temples, mulling over the current undertaking. With everyone's eyes on him, he began to pace back and forth again. After a few minutes, he paused, raised his head and looked around the room.

"Now," He said, his hands moving from his temples to join in a steeple at his chin, "What do we need for this?"

"How the hell are we supposed to know..." Kathleen started but Dan cut her off.

"Garbage bags, a sharp object, bleach, and duct tape," He said. Everyone turned to look at him, mouths agape. Dan stared back, dumbfounded, and shrugged, "What?"

"How the fuck do you know that?" Kathleen asked.

"It doesn't really matter how he knew, the fact of the matter is that he did know, and that makes it a little easier," Josh said, holding up a hand. He crossed the room and leaned in close to Dan, lowering his voice, "You answered that really quick... Are you sure?"

"Pretty sure," Dan replied. Josh nodded and walked to the kitchen to stand beside Kathleen. He and opened a few cupboards, moving the items inside around and peering inside.

"Run through that list again, Dan."

"Garbage bags, a sharp object, bleach, and duct tape." Josh continued rummaging through the already open cabinets before turning around. He put his hands on the kitchen counter and leaned next to Kathleen.

"Okay," Josh stated, tapping his fingers on the counter, "We have none of those things. First thing on the agenda is a grocery run. Who wants to go to the store?" No one moved. After a few beats, Josh slowly walked from the kitchen to the living room and picked up his keys.

"Then I guess I'll just go alone."

He reached out a hand towards the doorknob just as the pounding started on the apartment door. Josh stopped short, staring at the door and everyone else remained frozen, only allowing their eyes to widen. The pounding on the door came again. This time, Kristen pushed herself off of the couch with a frustrated sigh and moved forward to open the door. Josh, whose arm was already extended towards the doorknob, caught her arm and held up a finger.

"No one can get in without buzzing," he explained in a whisper. He knew that the person on the other side of the door couldn't hear him through the fire-resistant door, but he thought it was best to be safe, "The front entryway door is locked." He released Kristen's arm and slowly moved sideways across the room. He opened a drawer in his television stand and drew out a pistol.

"What the fuck is that for?" Kathleen hissed in a lowered voice, following Josh's lead.

"Protection," He said as he motioned for Kristen to open to the door. She cautiously placed her hand on the doorknob as Josh trained his gun on the door. She chewed her lower lip for a moment then glanced over her shoulder.

"Are you a good shot?" She asked quietly.

"Moderately," Josh whispered. Kristen scrunched up her face.

"When was the last time you practiced with that thing?"

"Just open the door!"

Kristen nodded. Her hand tightened around the doorknob, turning it slowly, then she yanked the door open.

Another Body

"Hey guys, someone left the downstairs door open, so I let myself up," Colleen stated as she entered the apartment, closing the door behind her. Josh quickly leaned on his television stand with the gun in his hand out of sight, "What are we up to?"

"Nothing at all," Andy spat, a little too quickly, as he plastered a smile on his sweaty face.

"What?" Asked Colleen, turning to Kristen with a quizzical look on her face. Kristen shook her head and walked towards the kitchen counter to take a seat on one of the stools.

Andy stood up from the futon and tossed his hands in the air, "Nothing. Nothing at all. What's with all the questions?"

Dan placed a hand over his mouth and tilted his head towards Andy as he whispered, "Way to be cool, Man."

"Shut the fuck up! You don't have to worry about prison!" Andy said. It was very apparent that Andy's lack of coolness was being quickly replaced by fear as his voice was growing louder with each word out of his mouth. Josh couldn't remember if he still had neighbors next door, but he didn't want to take any chances. He put his hands out, palms down, and crossed the room towards Andy.

"Andy," Josh said, "Buddy."

Andy started pacing the floor, yelling, "This shit wasn't even my fault! It wasn't even my idea! It wasn't even…"

"Andy, SIT THE FUCK DOWN!" Josh growled. Andy stopped mid-sentence and sat immediately on the floor where he had been standing just a few inches in front of the couch. Josh crouched before him, hands on his knees, looking him in the eyes, "Dude, we've known each other for a while and I've never seen you lose your cool. Ever. I don't want to see you lose your cool tonight. Alright?"

Andy nodded, sheepishly. Josh reached out and patted him on the shoulder. Andy closed his eyes and took in a deep, meditative breath. Then another. And another. His head sank down so his chin rested on his chest. Josh felt his shoulder relax, and he knew that they had gotten out of the woods. He turned his head to face the newcomer.

"What in the fuck is going on?" Colleen asked again. Josh winced, knowing full well that they were back at square one. Andy's head jerked up with a quick inhalation of air and his eyes went wide.

"AGAIN WITH THE FUCKING QUESTIONS?" He shrieked as he toppled over sideways to lay in the fetal position on the ground.

Josh stood up, shaking his head, and turned to face Colleen. That was when Drew popped up from behind the couch, rubbing his bloodshot eyes.

"What the fuck is with all the noise?" He shouted.

With a yelp, Josh instinctively spun around, raising his hand and clenching it into a fist in defense. Unfortunately, he had forgotten he was still holding the pistol. As his finger wrapped around the trigger the gun discharged with a deafening crack and Drew's head disappeared from sight, leaving only a spattering of red on the wall behind it. For a moment, Drew's headless body remained propped up behind the couch. Then there was a soft thud as the remainder it collapsed to the floor. Josh stood still, jaw slack and eyes wide, holding the smoking pistol in his hand. There was a moment of silence. Then Colleen screamed. After that, total chaos reigned supreme.

"You just shot his head completely off!" Kathleen yelled, her hands moving to the sides of her face. Josh's eyes went even wider as he looked from the crimson stain on his wall. He wheeled sideways towards Kathleen, who dropped behind the kitchen counter. Josh turned towards Colleen, who reeled backwards, slamming into the wall behind her. Her scream fizzled out into a whimper as she slid down the wall and landed on her ass on the floor with her hands in front of her face. Josh looked down at the gun in his hand, which he was now pointing towards the spot in the kitchen where Kathleen had been standing just a moment earlier. Without thinking, he released the gun, dropping it to the floor. His mouth began to move, trying to think of something to say, and he staggered backwards, until his legs hit the futon and landed sprawled across Dan's lap. He turned his head and looked up at Dan.

"I...I can't believe that just happened," Josh managed to muster in a shocked whisper. Dan, still staring at the bloody stain on the back of the couch with wide eyes, didn't move.

"Now we have two bodies to dispose of," he mumbled.

"How the fuck could you shoot Drew?" Kathleen asked from the kitchen floor. Josh looked in Kathleen's direction and motioned towards what was left of Drew as though she could see him from her hiding place behind the counter.

"What the hell was he doing behind the couch?" Josh screeched.

"What is Drew always doing?" Kathleen yelled back, "He was sleeping!"

"Why the fuck was he sleeping behind my couch?" Josh screamed. A hush fell over the room. It only lasted a few seconds before Andy, from his curled-up position on the floor, began to laugh. The group turned to stare at Andy in awe, Kathleen poking her head out from behind the counter. Andy didn't seem to notice, and if he did, he certainly didn't care. His laughter started out low but, in an instant, he tossed his head back, the laughter bursting out of him.

Dan and Josh made eye contact and Dan mouthed, *"He's finally lost it."* Josh could do nothing but nod. Andy went on laughing, sounding vaguely reminiscent of a psychotic version of Ricky Ricardo. He curled in on himself even further, holding his head in his hands. The laughing continued spilling out of him, harder and harder with each passing second. The harder he laughed, the louder the sound escalated and the higher pitch it became. After a few minutes, the laughter sounded exactly like that of a mad scientist. Kathleen moved her hands to her ears. Josh, Dan, and Colleen followed suit.

Kristen took matters into her own hands. She stood from her stool at the counter and stomped across the room. Leaning down, she grabbed Andy by his hair with both hands and yanked him upright, pulling his face close to hers. His high, menacing laugh changed quickly to a howl of pain. With a single slick, fluid motion, she moved her hand from his hair to his shirt and, with her other hand, she slapped him once, across the face, the connection almost as loud as the gunshot that had taken place just minutes previous, cutting his howl in half. A look of utter shock replaced the intense look of pain on Andy's face that had, in turn, replaced the look of insanity. Kristen leaned in close, grasping hold of Andy more securely by placing her slapping hand on his shirt as well. Andy turned his face towards Josh and Dan as he cowered back as best he could, but with Kristen's death grip on his shirt, he was unable to move very far.

"What are you laughing at?" She snarled, her lips curling back from her teeth. Andy winced as Kristen's warm breath played across his cheek.

"Because..." Andy started, gasping for breath, "...because..."

"Because what?" Kristen bellowed. Andy opened his eyes and looked up at Josh.

"Because, now I'll have a cell mate," He sputtered, voice cracking as he began braying laughter again. The look of horror was once again replaced by a look of complete craziness. Kristen grunted as she raised her hand to slap him again. She stopped herself, hand in mid-flight, when she realized that the laughter had multiplied. She shot a look at Josh, who had joined in with his own laughter, a nearly breathless gasp. Josh pointed at Andy, making him laugh even harder before Andy pointed back. Andy gasped for air, "You're my hero, Josh."

"We gotta have each other's backs," Josh cackled. Kristen's face had become a blank look of confusion. She released Andy's shirt and slowly backed away, sinking slowly to the couch. Andy crawled the few inches to lean against the futon where Josh was still sprawled across Dan's legs. They gave each other a high five, their breathing hitching in their throats. Josh then turned so his distorted clown smile was inches from the horrified Dan's face and raised a hand in the universal symbolic gesture of high-fiving, "Up top!"

Without thinking, Dan slapped Josh a high five, throwing Josh off balance and sending him falling backwards off of Dan's lap and onto the floor in a heap. This made Andy laugh even harder. Dan joined in, starting out soft and low but moving quickly to match the riotous laughter of both Josh and Andy. Tears were streaming down their faces as the two men watched Josh try to pick himself up off of the floor and fail due to the strain the laughing was putting on his muscles.

"What's going on?" Colleen asked softly from her spot against the wall. The laughter became chaotic.

Slowly, the laughter subsided into chuckling, then proceeded to boil down into random giggling before it ceased completely. When there was no more laughter, Josh pulled himself from the ground, removing his glasses and wiping the tears from his eyes. Kristen stormed up to him.

"You guys done?" She asked. Josh wiped a tear from his eye and nodded, allowing a final giggle to escape his mouth.

"I think so," he said, offering up a semi-apologetic smile.

"Good," Kristen said with zero emotion. She grasped hold of his arm and yanked him towards the door. With her free hand, she snatched his keys off of the hook on the wall and thrust them into his palm, "Now you and Dan are going to the store to get supplies." Josh held up his hands.

"Why do me and Dan have to go?" He asked, "Why can't you and Kathleen do it?"

"Because this isn't our apartment," Kathleen stated immediately, "And I still think this is a terrible idea." Josh blinked once but said no more. He grit his teeth and looked at Dan. Dan took this as his cue to stand up and get moving. He pushed himself up off the futon. The two grabbed their coats. Josh lit up a cigarette.

"You're driving," Josh said, setting his keys on top of his bookshelf, "I don't have insurance and I certainly don't want to get pulled over tonight." Dan looked at the clock.

"It's two in the morning," he said, "No place in Woodstock is open right now. Where are we going to go?"

"Meijer in McHenry," Josh stated, "It's forty minutes round trip. They have everything."

"No more funny business," Kristen growled, grabbing the two by the shoulders and spinning them around to face her., "Get going, unless you want to be caught with two dead bodies in your house." She bent to pick up the gun off of the floor and bumped into the television stand. Josh watched as a can of beer fell to the floor and began pouring out on the carpet. He brought his palm to his forehead and pointed at the beer.

"Man, you just spilled on my floor," He moaned. Kristen's jaw dropped and she furrowed her brow. She dramatically pointed at the bloodstain on the wall behind the couch and then equally emphatically at the bathroom that held the stab wound victim in the bathtub.

"Point taken," Josh said and nodded his head. Dan opened the front door and the two entered the hallway. The apartment fell silent again as Dan and Josh's footsteps faded down the hallway.

"What is going on?" Colleen asked, looking around the room. Kathleen stood from her spot on the kitchen floor and, grabbing a glass from the open cabinet, she poured two full glasses of vodka. She walked out of the kitchen and held a glass out to Colleen.

"Good thinking," Colleen whispered. They raised the glasses in a silent toast but before they could set their lips on the rim, Kristen put her hands over the top of the glasses. She looked from Kathleen to Colleen.

"Don't get too drunk," She said, "It's gonna be a long night."

The Drive

"Do you ever have that feeling that you're forgetting something?" Josh asked as they drove down the desolate country backroads, "But you can't figure out what it is?"

"All the time," Dan said, slamming on the brakes as they came up to a stop sign. After a beat, he gunned the engine and they tore off.

"I've got that right now," Josh said, shaking his head, "It's driving me nuts."

"It's probably just the double homicide that we're trying to cover up," Dan replied, "Hold on." He took a curve at a much faster pace than he should have. Dan's driving was, as usual, fast and loose. Under normal duress, Josh may have been nervous but, at this juncture, he didn't mind. He had the window rolled down, eyes closed, and his head leaned back against the seat. He was enjoying the ride, especially considering that the idea of the car skidding off the road, rolling into a ditch, and slamming full force into a tree, ending in a major explosion and a double DOA, actually seemed like a great way to escape the evening relatively unscathed. However, something was gnawing at the back of his brain and he couldn't quite put his finger on what it was. He figured that maybe Dan was right.

"Tonight is pretty well fucked up, huh?" Josh said.

"I never saw this coming," Dan responded.

"Me neither."

Josh opened his eyes and stared out the window, tapping his fingers on the door, keeping time with the song coming out of the speakers. There was something he was missing. Something he had forgotten. If he could only remember what it was. He stopped, cocking his head towards the speaker, before looking quizzically at Dan.

"Is this the Batman theme?" He asked, motioning towards the radio.

"Yes it is," Dan stated proudly, reaching out to crank the volume until was nearly deafening. He laid his foot to the pedal and the pedal to the floor. The trees whizzed by at a rapid pace and Josh secretly hoped that perhaps Dan was taking him to The Batcave, where he would unveil that he was, in fact, the Dark Knight, and the two of them would be off on some sort of adventure to save the city. The hopes were shattered when he saw the vibrant sign for the grocery store on the horizon.

As they pulled into the Meijer parking lot, Josh looked around, surprised to see that the lot was oddly filled for a Wednesday evening after two a.m. Dan managed to find a spot after circling the parking lot only once, and he killed the engine, cutting the music abruptly. The two sat in the car in complete silence for a few moments, staring straight ahead and listening to the clicks of the engine as it fell into a sound sleep. The tickle in Josh's brain reared its head. He narrowed his eyes, trying with all of his might to figure out what he had forgotten. Nothing came to him.

"I just wish I could remember what I forgot," Josh stated with a sigh. He reached down and unbuckled his seatbelt, "We should probably get this over with."

"Okay, you know what we need," Josh said, "Lead the way." Dan pointed to his right and they began making their way through the labyrinth of aisles. They arrived at the laundry aisle and stared at the shelves filled with bleach products. Josh stroked his chin, trying to decide what type of bleach they wanted to get.

"Do we want color guard bleach?" Josh asked.

"I think that we should just go with the biggest, cheapest bottle of bleach we can find," Dan replied. Josh raised mulled it over for a moment.

"I like that idea," he replied.

"Cheapness is a sense."

Dan reached out and grabbed a 64-ounce bottle with the word "Bleach" printed on it in block letters. He studied the word, turned the bottle in his hands, finding no more writing, and put it in the cart, "One down."

Josh turned around saw that garbage bags were directly behind them. Thank God for small favors. He reached out and grabbed a five pack of hefty bags. Dan shook his head.

"I think we should get a different pack," he said. Josh looked at the box in his hand and then pointed at the writing on the front.

"Super Durable. We should stick with these," he said, "Durability. We don't want the bags to break, do we? That would be awful."

"No," Dan said, "But we should get more bags."

"More bags?" Josh asked, slightly shocked, "But there are only two bodies."

"It's your call," Dan said with a shrug. Josh looked at the bags and then back at Dan. He decided that Dan, who seemed to have a strangely acute knowledge on the subject of disposing of bodies, was probably right, so he tossed the bags back on the shelf and grabbed the economy pack.

"Better to be safe," Dan stated, "Now, we need something sharp."

"I've got knives and razors at my house," Josh said, "No need to spend money on things we already have." Dan shook his head, immediately washing away any feelings of worth that Josh had in this situation.

"We're gonna need something that can cut through harder materials," Dan said. Josh looked at him with a blank stare.

"I've got my swiss army knife," he said cautiously. Dan shook his head.

"It needs to cut through very hard material."

"You used my swiss army knife to cut through an aluminum can before," Josh pointed out. Dan rolled his eyes. He looked around the aisle to make sure they were alone and then leaned in and cupped his hand to Josh's ear.

"We need something that can cut through bone."

"Ahhhh."

Dan motioned and began moving towards the hardware department, Josh followed quickly on his heels. Once they reached the hardware department, Dan picked up the biggest hacksaw he could find. He placed the saw in Josh's hand and Josh looked at it closely, turning it over in his hands, studying the saw.

"This should do quite nicely," Josh said finally, handing the saw back to Dan.

"Do you know a lot about tools?" Dan asked.

"No," Josh stated honestly, "I just assumed that if I looked at the saw enough it would make it seem like I knew what the hell I was talking about. Truth be told, you could've handed me a squeegee and I would've done the same thing." With that, Josh walked down the aisle in search of duct tape. Dan walked behind him.

"Three pack should do." He said. Dan agreed.

"Do we have everything we need," Josh asked.

"Duct tape, garbage bags, bleach, and saw," Dan said, taking inventory, "Looks like we have everything we need."

"All right then, let's get out of here!" Josh exclaimed. With Dan leading the way, the two began to march towards the checkers, happy that the night would soon be over. That was when Josh's brain finally let loose the information that he had been trying to recall. He stopped short in the middle of the aisle, his face draining of color.

"Oh my god," he said.

Dan stopped as well, looking back over his shoulder at Josh, "What?"

With a worried look spreading quickly across his face, Josh patted his back pockets. From there he proceeded to pat his front pockets, his jacket pockets, and his shirt pockets before returning his hands to his back pockets to double check. The end result was the same however as he let loose a string of profanity under his breath.

"I forgot my wallet."

"How could you forget your wallet?" Dan groaned with a roll of his eyes. Josh stared at Dan in disbelief.

"Are you serious?" He snapped, "Maybe there was too much going on in my apartment. Y'know, what with the dead body in my bathroom and the fact that a guy's head exploded in mist, leaving brain and skull spattered on my walls. Maybe my mind wasn't exactly in proper clear thinking mode. What do you think?"

"That's probably a pretty good assumption."

Josh ran his hands through his hair, first going back and then moving them forwards. He took a deep breath and let it out slowly.

"Do you have any money, Dan?" He asked, already knowing the answer before he even formulated the question.

"I don't even have a job, remember?" Dan pointed out, shaking his head. Josh patted his pockets again, as if, by checking a second time, his wallet would magically appear. Dan leaned against the cart.

"Great."

"What are we gonna do?" Dan asked, "It's kind of a haul to go all the way back to your apartment and then come all the way back here."

"I completely agree," Josh said, "Considering that it is already almost three and we should really be disposing of bodies by the cover of night, there's really only one thing we can do in this situation."

"Which is?"

"We steal it."

Back at the Apartment

Kathleen, standing in the kitchen at the counter, handed a shot glass to Colleen as she brought her own to her lips. The majority of the vodka spilled down the front of Colleen's shirt but, considering that it was their twelfth consecutive shot, it was fairly impressive that she managed to get even a portion of the shot in her mouth, which hadn't been a problem with the last eleven shots. Colleen was leaning against the kitchen wall in a poor attempt to maintain at least a semblance of stability and Kathleen was paying absolutely no attention to her at this point.

For Kathleen, the entire world revolved around the mostly filled second bottle of Smirnoff before her and the shot glass in her hand. The apartment, including the two dead bodies and three very much alive ones, had almost completely ceased to exist. She figured that, over the course of the remainder of the bottle, the nightmare she was currently in would cease to exist entirely and that was exactly what she wanted at this point.

Kristen sat across from Kathleen, with her elbows on the counter and her hand resting the gun that lay before her. She sat in silence, a deep, brooding silence. Under normal duress, one of the other people in the room may have asked her what was on her mind. However, she had a wild look in her eyes and, coupled with the weapon at her fingertips and the events that had previously taken place, so everyone left her to her own devices.

Andy slowly rose from his spot on the couch and made his way to the kitchen. He brushed past Colleen, steadying her as she began to slip sideways, and took a glass from the open cabinet. Without a word, he crossed back through the kitchen and settled onto the stool beside Kristen.

"Pour me one of those," he said, holding out the glass. Kathleen didn't even bother to look up from her own glass. She picked up the vodka bottle and began pouring, either unaware or beyond caring that Andy's glass was nowhere near her. The vodka spilled from the bottle onto the counter top, where it collected in a puddle and slowly trickled to the floor. Andy didn't comment. He merely moved his glass in place, waited until it was filled, then said, "Okay, that's good."

Kathleen moved the still upturned bottle to her own glass, spilling more vodka on the counter in the process which, in turn, spilled to the floor. Once her glass was filled again, she moved the bottle to the shot glass in Colleen's hand, bypassing the counter altogether as she poured the liquor directly on the floor. Colleen pulled her cup away, knocking Kathleen's hand in the process. The vodka spilled from the mouth of the bottle onto Colleen's shirt. Neither woman seemed to notice. Kathleen held the bottle the for a few moments, pouring the liquid on Colleen and nearly soaking her completely, before up right-ing the bottle and replacing it beside her on the counter. She raised her glass jerkily. Andy followed suit.

"Here'sh to prishon," She slurred. With a quick motion, she raised her head and the glass simultaneously. The liquor disappeared into her mouth and down her throat. Kathleen slammed her glass down on the counter and let her head loll down again. Andy brought his glass up, polished off the drink, and slammed his down as well. Colleen, on the other hand, attempted to move her mostly empty glass to her lips but, as she reached the midway point, she slid down the wall, and collapsed in a heap on the floor in the puddle of booze that had been spilled.

Kristen, concentration broken by the soft thud of Colleen falling to the ground, was pulled back to the reality of the apartment around her. She glanced down at Colleen, then slammed her hand down on the counter.

"That's it," She hissed, "Enough is enough." She leaned forward and grabbed the vodka bottle by the neck. While her intention had been to throw the bottle at the wall, smashing it to pieces and disposing of the remainder of the liquor, she never got that far. Without moving her head, Kathleen's hand shot out, instinctively, like a mongoose and gripped the bottle tight. Kristen gave the bottle a tug, trying in vain to wrench it from Kathleen's grip. Kathleen's grip was like a vice.

"Gimme that bottle," Kristen growled.

"Fuck you," Kathleen snarled back, never lifting her chin from her chest. With a swift yank, she tore the bottle from Kristen's grasp and held it to her chest like a baby. Kristen gritted her teeth. Her hand tightened on the gun beneath it. Pulling the pistol up, she cocked it and held it to Kathleen's hairline.

"Give me the bottle," Kristen stated coolly. Kathleen raised her head slowly and the barrel of the gun traced down her forehead and came to a rest between her weary eyes. The eyes sluggishly followed suit, moving from the glass on the counter to the gun in her face, then back down to the cherished bottle against her bosom. Kristen leaned forward further, pressed the gun harder into Kathleen's head. Kathleen winced in pain but hesitated for a moment longer before defeatedly holding out the bottle. Kristen snatched it from her and took the gun from her face, "I asked you not to get too fucked up."

"I'm not fucked up," Kathleen spat. She glared at Kristen icily. Kristen was about to retort when Kathleen opened her mouth, extended her tongue, and then lowered her head to the kitchen counter and began to lap up the spilled contents before her with all the table manners of a stray dog. Kristen could do nothing but stare at her. At first, her stare was quizzical as she was not completely sure what was going on but it quickly turned to disgust. Kathleen slowly raised her hand up, middle finger extended, and held it up to Kristen. Kathleen, with her face planted on the counter, did not see Kristen's face change for the third time. The disgust was replaced by rage and Kathleen was in mid-lick when Kristen's hand slammed into the back of her head, smashing her face against the counter before tightening and grabbing a handful of her hair. With a yank, Kristen snapped Kathleen's head up, drops of blood and vodka spraying across the counter. Kathleen was only able to let out a partial shriek of pain as the nerve endings had time to register both her broken nose and her hair being pulled before Kristen's right hook, still clutching the gun in her hand, caught Kathleen on the bridge of her already busted nose. A spray of blood shot from her nose and she reeled backwards, the back of her head connected with the corner of the open cabinet door behind her and she crumpled to the floor. A pool of blood began to seep out around her head like a halo. Kristen stood above her, shaking her throbbing hand.

"The hits just keep on coming," she muttered, looking at Kathleen's unconscious body on the ground. She shook her head. Out of the corner of her eye, she sensed movement. She cocked her head to the side and watched as Andy slowly reached out, in a poor attempt at stealth, and inched the vodka bottle towards himself. With a growl, Kristen spun around, lashing out and slapping his hand. Andy let loose a squeal and immediately retracted, wobbling on his stool and holding his hand against his chest. He looked at Kristen with a furrowed brow as he massaged his hurt hand.

"What'd you do that for?"

Change of Plans

"Really?" Dan asked Josh, not trying to hide the surprise in his voice, "You think we should just walk out without paying?" Josh nodded, not slowing his pace. They had been walking around the store aimlessly for fifteen minutes as they tried to decide the best way to deal with the problem at hand.

"The thing is," Josh said, coming to a stop and turning to look at Dan, "If we're going to do this, we may as well make the best of it, right?"

"Wait a second," Dan whispered harshly, "Are you saying we should take more."

"That is absolutely what I am saying," Josh said, "Go big or go home, that's what I always say."

"I've never heard you say that," Dan replied.

"I always say that."

Josh turned the corner and walked down the liquor aisle. He ran his fingers along the shelves as he walked. Stopping, he picked up a bottle of Grey Goose Vodka and held it in the crook of his arm. He walked a little further, grabbed a handle of Jack Daniels and Captain Morgan. He continued in this manner, walking along and picking up other liquor products as he went.

"Hey, we really shouldn't be doing this," Dan said, "After a certain amount this becomes a felony."

"Three hundred dollars," Josh said, depositing an armful of bottles into the cart. Dan counted up the amount of alcohol in the cart and then did a quick calculation in his head.

"We have over three hundred right now," Dan said. He pointed to the top shelf, "Grab the Jager."

"You got it."

"Seriously, man," Dan continued, shaking his head, "We can't do this. This place has some serious security, this is gonna land us in the slammer, and then they'll find the bodies and we'll spend a lot longer than we want to in jail. What about beer, should we get beer?"

"Yeah," Josh said, "Definitely beer." He grabbed a thirty case. Hesitated. Then grabbed a second one for good measure. He took one last look down the aisle and motioned towards the exit.

"I'll say it one last time," Dan said, looking around to make sure that there was no one coming for them, "We should really just leave."

"You're right," Josh said, grabbing the front of the cart and motioning towards the exit, "Shall we?"

"So much for good intentions," Dan said with a sigh. He began pushing the cart, "Let's get the hell out of here."

"We get one shot," Josh said as they strode towards the front of the store, "We can't fuck this up." The door was coming closer now. Neither Josh nor Dan wanted to look around. They kept their eyes glued to the door. It was only a few more steps and then they would be free.

"Dan?"

Dan and Josh both froze. They turned simultaneously to find themselves looking at a pretty young woman holding a bag of cat food. They looked at each other as the Brooke moved towards them.

"What are the odds?" Josh muttered to Dan, "Just act naturally."

"Got it," Dan whispered back. He turned to the woman, raising his voice, and extending his arms for a hug, "Heeeey, Brooke. What are you doing here?"

"I couldn't sleep," Brooke said, smiling, as she moved in to give Dan a hug, "I needed to get cat food anyway so I figured I'd take a drive."

"Good idea," Dan said, "What are you up to?"

"Not much," Brooke said, raising an eyebrow, "Like I said, I just needed to get cat food. Where are you headed?"

"This is Josh. We're going to Josh's apartment," Dan said, hooking a thumb towards Josh. Josh smiled and gave a little wave. Brooke nodded back. Dan nodded as well and, before he was even aware it was happening, his instinct kicked in, "Do you want to come over?"

Josh's eyes flew open and a gasp escaped from his mouth as he shot Dan a look. It took everything in his power not to slap his forehead with his palm. Dan looked back, eyes equally wide and a shocked look on his face. Brooke glanced down at her watch and didn't seem to notice.

"Sure," Brooke said, giddily, "I just gotta grab a few more things. Can I meet you there in about an hour?"

"Totally," Dan said with another nod. He grinned at Brooke, trying to hide the sheer terror that he knew his eyes were conveying. It must've been working because Brooke smiled back before turning and walking away from them. As soon as her back was turned, Dan spun towards Josh with a horrified look on his face. Josh stared at Dan in disbelief.

"What was that?" Josh asked, motioning angrily towards Brooke.

"I don't know what happened," Dan stammered, "I went on auto-pilot!"

"I could stab you right now," Josh said, trying to maintain his calm, "Seriously."

"You're the one that said act natural!" Dan retorted.

"I meant act natural in the sense of 'don't draw attention to us'," Josh hissed, "I didn't mean to invite someone to a crime scene."

"That was how I act natural," Dan said, "Maybe you should've been a bit more clear with your instructions."

Josh's lips began moving, though he could not force words out. All he could do was make clicking sound with his throat and blink his eyes. Dan looked at him, puzzled, wondering if Josh had finally had a break down.

"Car," Josh blurted, louder than he had anticipated. He took a deep breath, regaining his composure, "Let's just get to the car." He turned on his heels and walked out the front door as quickly as possible with Dan pushing the cart behind him.

The crisp night air was a welcome relief as they made their way out of the blinding fluorescent lights. When they reached to the car, Dan opened his trunk and they began tossing the contents of the cart inside. Once everything was inside, Dan slammed the trunk closed. Josh shoved the empty cart across the parking lot and the two turned to get into the car. For the first time all evening, Josh had the feeling that everything was going to turn out okay.

"Excuse me. Sir?"

"Fuck," Josh breathed. The voice came from behind them and when Josh turned around to see an obese, balding man with a goatee abounding across the parking lot toward them. He could tell by the look of seriousness plastered across his face that this man meant business. Josh had no doubt that it was the store manager.

"I knew this was going to happen," Dan said, shooting a glare at Josh, "Didn't I tell you this was going to happen?"

"Calm down," Josh said, holding up a finger, "I'll handle this. Just start the car." He walked briskly around the car and met the manager midway across the parking lot as Dan slipped into the driver's seat.

"Hey, bud," Josh called out, "What can I do for you?"

The manager stopped walking and crossed his thick arms over his meaty chest. His already serious face took on an additional layer that would've made any high school principal jealous.

"I need you and your buddy to come back inside."

"Us?" Josh asked, letting a mask of confusion cross his face, "What seems to be the problem?" The manager stood with his legs planted firmly at shoulder's length apart. His face didn't move a muscle. It was very clear that he was not interested in any shenanigans.

"I think you and I both know the answer to that question, son," He stated.

"If I knew the answer, I wouldn't be asking," Josh replied. He knew that there were only two options to get out of this scenario. Option one was to stick to his convictions. However, the manager was also willing to stand his ground.

"Look, Pal," he said, "I know you left the store without paying for the merchandise you had. If you come back in, we can deal with this easily. We'll just call the police and we'll get this all sorted out."

"You haven't called the police yet?" Josh asked, moderate surprise creeping into his voice. The manager shook his head. Josh knew that it was clearly time for Option two. Without hesitation, he threw a harsh kick between the manager's legs, his foot connecting squarely with the manager's balls. With a yelp of surprise, the big man immediately doubled over, toppling towards the ground, cupping his crotch in his hands. Before the manager had hit the pavement, Josh was already leaping into the passenger side of the car.

"Drive, dammit!" he yelled as he was closing the door. Dan didn't ask questions. His foot hit the gas, the car peeled out, leaving the manager in the parking lot, writhing on the ground and holding his incredibly sore testicles.

Andy was back on the futon. Kristen was now seated opposite him, on the couch, holding the gun in her hands. She kept it trained on Andy. With a sigh of irritation, Andy held up his hands.

"I'm not gonna go for the Vodka again, I swear," he said, "Jesus." Kristen gritted her teeth and winced.

"You know damn well that this isn't about the Vodka, Andy."

"If this is about what I think this is about, you already have my word," Andy said. Kristen cocked the hammer of the gun. Andy closed his eyes and shrank back against the futon.

"You better keep..." She stopped mid-sentence as the front door swung open. She was on her feet immediately, wheeling towards the door, gun trained on the doorway. Josh stepped through the doorway, saw Kristen holding the gun, and leapt backwards, returning to the hallway. Kristen lowered the gun.

"Don't shoot," Josh's voice wafted around the corner, "It's just us."

"Josh and Dan," Dan clarified.

"I know that now," she said with a sigh, "Get in here." There was no movement in the doorway, though Kristen could hear some hushed whispering.

"Andy?" Josh called. Andy looked at Kristen who motioned at the gun. Andy turned his head towards the door.

"She has the gun but it's at her side," He called, "You're safe."

Josh's hand popped through the doorway and quickly disappeared. A second later, the hand reappeared and waved. When it didn't get shot off, Josh and Dan decided that the coast was clear. They walked through the doorway, their arms filled with all of the stolen merchandise from the car. Dan shut the door behind him with his foot and they dropped all of the stuff on the couch. Dan sat down next to it, breathing heavily. Kristen's jaw dropped.

"What the hell is all of this?" She asked shrilly, waving the gun at the pile on the couch, "And why are you all sweaty?" Dan didn't verbalize an answer, he merely pointed at Josh. Kristen's eyes moved to Josh.

"We had a little incident at the store," Josh explained, "I made Dan park a few blocks away so that the car couldn't be traced to my apartment." He made his way to the kitchen and saw Colleen and Kathleen sprawled out on the floor. He spun around towards Kristen.

"The body count wasn't high enough?" He asked.

"They're not dead," Kristen said, "I checked."

"They certainly look dead," Josh pointed at Kathleen, "She's all bloody."

"She punched her in the face," Andy spat. Kristen turned and shot Andy a warning look.

"What the hell did you do that for?" Josh asked.

"I punched Kathleen because she was getting out of control," Kristen said.

Josh motioned towards Colleen, "And what about her?"

"The result of Kathleen getting out of control."

Josh bent down and felt for a pulse on Colleen. He sniffed at the air and quickly rose to his feet, "Good Lord, she's really drunk."

"I know," Kristen told him.

"How much did you guys drink while we were gone?" Josh asked. He started to walk further into the kitchen and slipped, catching himself on the counter before he fell. He glanced down at his hand, shaking off the droplets of moisture. Then he looked at the ground, "Why is everything all wet?"

"We've already wasted enough time, so let's not do the small talk thing," Kristen said. She placed the gun in her waistband, "Let's get rid of that body in your bathroom."

"And the one behind my couch," Josh said. He walked to the couch and slapped Dan on the shoulder, "Get a move on, man, you're in charge of this part of the night."

"Forget it," Dan said, "I need to rest for a few minutes."

Josh closed his eyes and rubbed a hand down his face, "Considering that you are the one who apparently knows what the hell he is doing, you gotta move."

"All you do is cut up the body and put it in the garbage bags," Dan explained, "Then you close the bags with duct tape and we get rid of the body parts. How hard is that?" Josh shrugged, he looked at Kristen.

"I think that the two of us can handle that," he said. Kristen nodded in agreement, "But we have to move fast. Dan invited someone over."

Kristen set her jaw. She crossed the floor and slapped Dan in the back of the head. Dan didn't bother to argue, he knew he deserved it. He shrugged his shoulders, "He told me to act naturally."

"Sometimes I wonder about you," Kristen said. She turned, with a flip of her hair, and motioned for Josh to follow her to the bathroom. Josh grabbed the saw, the bags, and the duct tape and made his way to the bathroom. Kristen paused before entering and pointed at Andy, "You better keep your mouth shut." Andy nodded as Kristen and Josh disappeared into the bathroom, closing the door behind them.

As soon as they were gone, Andy turned to Dan.

"Dude, I gotta tell you something."

In the Bathroom with the Body

The bathroom was a disaster.

It was a small bathroom to begin with and now it was filled to beyond capacity with three people, two living and one dead. Kristen and Josh stood inches apart as they surveyed the scene. The floor and baseboards were covered in spatters of blood. The glass shower door was broken. One of the cabinet doors hung by one hinge. The toilet lit was cracked and sat askew. The mirror above the sink was shattered. Josh ran his fingers through his hair and chewed on his bottom lip.

"I am definitely not getting my security deposit back," he muttered. Kristen tapped her watch.

"Time is of the essence," she said, "Let's get a move on." Josh looked at the bloodied body of Dave laying in the bathtub amidst the broken glass.

"At least he's already in the shower," Josh said, "Thank god for small miracles."

"Yeah," Kristen replied, "clean up will be a little easier."

"Lifting him would've been a bitch. He's nothing but dead weight," Josh said, "Although, he was really nothing but dead weight before this happened." Kristen disregarded his comment.

Josh sat down on the broken toilet lid. He stared at the lifeless form that was Dave. Kristen crossed her arms.

"Where do we start?" She asked.

Josh didn't answer. He stared at Dave for a few seconds longer before turning to Kristen, "What did you see in this guy?"

"Seriously?" Kristen was taken aback by this question. She held her hands out at her sides, "We're gonna have this conversation now?"

"I'm just curious," Josh said, grabbing the saw and standing. He stepped into the tub, straddling the body, and grabbed ahold of Dave's hand. Lifting Dave's arm up, he placed the saw blade into the crook of the elbow and started to cut.

"You can't help who you're attracted to," Kristen said. Josh nodded as a spray of blood hit his face. Instantaneously, he vomited. He turned his head to the side.

"This is grotesque," he choked.

"You can say that again."

Andy looked across the room at the bathroom door, hesitating for a moment before he scurried across the room to sit beside Dan on the couch. He glanced at the bathroom door again and then moved closer to Dan, motioning for Dan to lend him an ear. Dan leaned his head towards Andy's mouth. Andy checked the bathroom door again, looked quickly around the room at the two unconscious bodies in the kitchen and the headless body spilling out from behind the couch.

"Okay," he said when he was sure there was no listening ears in the room, "Kristen threatened to kill me if I told anyone this, so I gotta be short and quick." He looked around the room again and one word came thrashing into Dan's mind. Paranoia.

"I didn't kill Dave," Andy whispered into Dan's ear, "Kristen did." He breathed a sigh of relief as he leaned back into the couch, holding up his hands. Dan remained leaning towards him, thinking that Andy was going to offer some sort of further explanation. When he realized that Andy had said everything he was going to say, he threw his hands in the air as well.

"What the hell are you talking about?" Dan asked. Andy put his hands up even further.

"I didn't kill the guy," he stated bluntly, "Kristen saw an opportunity and she took it. I took the rap. That's all."

"When the hell did this all happen?"

"Remember when Kristen took me out in the hall earlier?" Andy asked. Dan slowly nodded. Though his mind was a bit hazy with everything going on, he had a vague recollection of Kristen and Andy disappearing for a short while. Andy cocked his head to the side, "When she took me into the hall, she told me that she had slit Dave's throat. Apparently, all of us weren't paying attention, we were all too busy drinking and having a good time. She told me that I should take the rap because he had offended me earlier in the night with his racial slurs. So, I did it."

"But," Dan shook his head, trying to process the information, "Why did she kill Dave?"

Andy shrugged, "If I knew that, then this would be a whole lot easier on my mind. I have no idea. In all honesty, can you blame her."

Dan contemplated for a moment. As he replayed his interaction's with Dave, remembering the man's comments and behavior throughout the night, he was surprised that he could come up with no reason why anyone in the world would not want to kill Dave.

"I'm actually surprised this didn't happen to him sooner," Dan concluded.

"Me too," Andy said, closing his eyes, "Me too."

The two sat in silence for a moment. Then Dan cocked his head to the side. He looked at Andy.

"Wait," He said, "If Kristen was the culprit the whole time, why did you seem so worried?" Andy smiled and nodded.

"She asked me to play it up," Andy said, "And you know how much I love theatrics."

Kathleen Wakes Up

Kathleen's eyes fluttered open and she found herself looking at the underside of a cabinet. For a moment, she had no idea what had happened. She rolled herself to her side, wincing at the sharp and throbbing pain that was emanating from both the front and back sides of her head. When she saw the blood on the floorboards before her, the night's events came fluttering back to her and she was immediately pissed off.

"I'm gonna kill that bitch," She mumbled.

Though she wanted immediate results, she couldn't get up from the floor right away. The room was spinning like a vortex in front of her and for a moment, she thought she was going to loose what little she had in her stomach She realized that the contents of her stomach was mostly liquid in nature and she found herself thankful that she had drank as much as she did because she knew full well that her broken nose and lacerated scalp would have hurt a whole lot worse if she hadn't. The feeling of nausea passed and she slowly dragged herself from the floor with the unease of turtle on its back. She reached her hands up and, grasping the edge of the sink, pulled herself up to a standing position. Her knees were wobbly, so she stood still, head bent forward, staring down at the dirty dishes before her. She watched as blood dripped from her nose onto curdled milk that was congealed in the cereal bowls.

"Fuck."

She blinked her eyes as she started to turn away from the sink. Then the black handled butcher's knife caught her attention. She stopped, mid-turn. A hint of a smile fell across her lips as she moved her hands into the sink and grasped the knife by the handle. She delicately pulled the knife from the menagerie of dishes before her, unsheathing the silver, marinara encrusted blade. She turned away from the sink and, taking baby steps across the bloodied, vodka-soaked floor, stumbled towards the living room.

Unexpected

"Can you hand me a towel?" Josh asked. He had not realized that the human body acted as a geyser when it was being dismembered. The sprays of blood had managed to cover his face and body almost completely and he could no longer wipe the mess away from his face with his bloodied hands. Every time he tried to do so, all he managed to do was smear the bloody mask around.

"Where's the towel?" Kristen asked as she reached behind her towards the towel rack and found nothing. Josh pointed blindly over her shoulder.

"It's on the towel rack," He stated. Kristen shook her head before she realized Josh couldn't see her non-verbal communication.

"No, it's not," she said.

"Then hand me some a tissue or some toilet paper or something," Josh sighed, "I can't see a fucking thing." Kristen reached out and knocked the empty tissue box to the floor. She maneuvered her hand and reached for the roll of toilet paper. Her fingers landed upon an empty cardboard tube.

"You're out of toilet paper."

"What the fuck?" Josh growled, "How is that even possible? I had a whole roll like two hours ago."

Kristen shrugged, "Well, you don't have a whole roll now. You don't have any."

"God dammit!" Josh yelled. His irritation had reached a boiling point. He tried again, fruitlessly, to wipe the blood from his face with his bloodied hands, "Get me something! Anything! I'm fucking blind over here."

"I'm going to go see if you have any paper towels in the kitchen," Kristen said, tugging open the bathroom door, "I'll be right back."

"Hurry up about it," Josh ordered, "I need to be able to see what I'm doing if I'm gonna finish this shit."

Kristen reached into the shower and flipped the water on. The shower sprang to life, spraying Josh in ice cold water. He yelped. Kristen smiled to herself.

"That should help."

"**S**hould we say something about it?" Dan asked. Andy jerked upright and his eyes went wide. He looked at Dan and shook his head.

"Uhh... No," He said, "Absolutely fucking not."

"Why?"

"How about because she would kill me."

"How do you know that's not an empty threat?"

Andy motioned towards the closed bathroom door. Dan glanced at the door, remembering the recently murdered body, and nodded slowly, "Point well taken."

"What we gotta do," Andy stated, closing his eyes and rubbing his temples, "Is to make damn sure that we get the hell out of here alive. We'll deal with any repercussions later on down the road. Kristen killed Dave. She certainly wouldn't have any qualms about killing me."

Dan's foot barked across Andy's shin. Andy opened his eyes and reached down, grasping his leg. He looked down to see if there was a bruise forming.

"What the fuck was that for, douchebag?" He hissed as he raised his face towards Dan. He paused for a moment when his gaze landed on Dan's face. Dan's eyes were wider than they had ever been in his life and Andy was almost certain that Dan had stopped breathing altogether. Andy furrowed his brow, "What's wrong with you?"

Dan's body didn't move at all, but his eyes flicked to the right several times in rapid fire succession., motioning for Andy to look beyond his huge eyes. Andy allowed his eyes to move slowly away from Dan, over his shoulder, and he found himself looking at the bathroom door. The door that was now opened. Andy's breath caught in his throat as he saw Kristen standing in the doorway, a cold glare fixed on Andy. She didn't have to say anything. Andy could feel the rage emanating from her and he knew that, if he didn't play his cards right, he was inches from death.

"Dan guessed," Andy shouted, "I didn't say a God damned thing and Dan guessed. He figured it out, he was like Sherlock Holmes, this guy." Kristen still didn't utter a word. She merely stepped forward and began to advance on Andy.

Andy bolted up from the couch. He stood, looking around the room, trying to figure out where he could run to in the studio apartment. The only exit wasn't an option as Kristen was less than a foot away from the front door and moving towards Andy like an alligator. There was no escape. Impulsively, he backed away from her, not realizing that he was backing himself into a corner.

"You son of a bitch," Kristen breathed, "Didn't I warn you?" She quickened her pace as she moved closer to Andy, reaching for the gun in her waistband as she did. Andy did the first thing that came to his mind.

He closed his eyes and prayed that death found him quickly.

Accidental Massacre

Kathleen, walking like a baby deer, had almost made it to the edge of the kitchen. Her head was still throbbing and there was a ringing in her ears so everything sounded faded and far away. She heard the bathroom door open. She heard the faint voices in the living room cease for a single beat, followed by Andy rambling off a line of excuses just before he entered her line of vision. When she heard Kristen's voice, she knew that she had a chance and she had to take it.

As soon as Kristen moved into her sight line, a rush of adrenaline knocked the alcohol haze and the concussion down a few notches. Kathleen moved like a wild cat, slowly at first moving stealthy across the kitchen floor. She sized up her opponent and, with a blood curdling roar of anger, she raised the knife in her hand and pounced.

Had Kathleen remained silent as she leapt, Kristen, who's periphery had been clouded with rage as she zeroed in on Andy, would've never heard her coming. Kathleen would've buried the knife all the way to the hilt deep in Kristen's spine and that would've been the end of that. However, Kathleen did roar. When Kristen heard the roar of fury, she was snapped out of her trance. She wheeled around, surprised, and momentarily forgot about the gun in her waistband and the terrified Andy in front of her. Her hand darted up just in time to grab hold of Kathleen's wrist and keep the knife away from her body.

Kathleen's momentum carried her forward, even though the arm holding the knife had ceased movement altogether. She crashed into Kristen, full force, sending both of them toppling to the floor in a heap of flailing limbs and angry murmurs.

Kathleen, in her anger, looked slightly reminiscent of a rabid badger. Her lips were pulled back across her teeth in a snarl of pure hate and anger and her eyes burned harshly with insanity. She wriggled around, trying in vain to move the knife close enough to Kristen's body to cut her. Although Kristen was able to maneuver out of the way of every attempt, Kathleen didn't seem to tire. The adrenaline pumping through her body mixed with the anger that was boiling in her blood kept her on high alert.

Kristen, knowing full well that she was not going to be able to subdue Kathleen for very much longer, allowed Kathleen's hand to move a few inches towards her. Kathleen saw that she was drawing closer with the knife blade and, for an instant, she thought that she was going to be victorious. She focused all of her energy on the arm holding the knife, letting down her guard for a split second, and that was all that Kristen needed. She bucked with her hips, tossing Kathleen sideways off of her. Kathleen rolled once on the carpet, crashed into the wall, and landed on the floor. Kristen stood up fast, but Kathleen scrambled to her feet faster, knife held low at her side, snarl still set upon her face. Kathleen and Kristen stood, staring each other down.

"What the fuck is wrong with you two?" Dan yelled. He stepped over the back of the couch, trying to put himself between the two warriors, "You're acting like a couple of assholes. Knock it the fuck off."

Neither Kristen nor Kathleen payed any attention to Dan. Their eyes and minds were focused only on one another. Kathleen moved first. Dan's feet got wrapped up in Drew's corpse and he pitched forward. Kathleen struck out at shoulder level with the knife.

Although she was aiming for Kristen, the knife blade never found its intended target. Instead, the knife, moving on a straightforward path, caught Dan in the neck as he fell forward. It sliced easily through his skin and muscle before puncturing his windpipe. For a moment, Kathleen could do nothing but stand completely motionless, holding Dan's wheezing body up, mid-topple, by the knife blade in his throat. Dan blinked his widened eyes. His lips started moving, but no sound came out. Kathleen, all thoughts of extracting vengeance upon Kristen gone from her mind, gasped and stepped quickly backwards, letting go of the knife. Dan toppled forwards, his body jerking slightly, and he landed on the floor with a thud. The blood began to pool out of his neck and around his head.

"Holy shit," Kathleen whimpered. She stood, staring down at Dan's body. Her face pale, "I... I just killed Dan."

"Holy shit," She said again. She broke down, tears streaming down her face. She lifted her face and pointed an accusing finger at Kristen, "That was your fault. That was meant for you."

Kathleen screamed, blood returning to her pale face at a rapid pace, changing the color from ashen gray to blood red in a matter of seconds. She lunged towards Kristen, head lowered and arms out to her side like a charging bull. With the grace of a dancer, Kristen pulled the gun from her waistband and side-stepped Kathleen's lunge. As Kathleen passed by her, Kristen brought the butt of the gun down on the base of her skull like a hammer. There was a sickening wet cracking sound as Kathleen's brain hit the front of her skull. Her momentum carried her onward a few more steps before she crashed head long into the bookshelf. The bookshelf tilted, spilling books everywhere and Kathleen fell with them. She lay motionless in the pile of books.

Andy, who had, up to this point, been standing motionless behind the couch, came back to life. The spell of Andy's initial terror was broken by his own desire for survival as he watched Kristen swiftly take Kathleen out. He took a deep breath and he knew he had to make a move while Kristen's back was still to him. Without thinking, he picked up the computer monitor from Josh's desk. He lifted it above his head and moved towards Kristen. He was a foot away when Kristen turned towards him, gun drawn and aimed directly at his chest. Andy froze.

"Shit," Andy muttered.

"I told you to keep your mouth shut," Kristen growled, "That was all you had to do, but you couldn't do that. Then you try to attack me while my back is turned? You've signed your own death certificate twice over, Andy."

Kristen motioned with the gun, telling Andy to back up. Andy glared at her but didn't move immediately. Kristen knew exactly what he was thinking. She shook her head, "Andy, even if you could throw that monitor hard enough to do any damage that I couldn't dodge, keep in mind that a bullet moves at 700 feet a second. If you want to try, go ahead, but let's just say that the odds are in my favor."

Andy realized that Kristen had made a pretty good point. He stepped backwards. He suddenly realized that, now that his adrenaline had been washed away, the monitor he was holding above his head was heavier than he had thought. His arms started to shake as he took another step back. Kristen stared him down. "Can I at least put the monitor down?" He asked. Kristen shook her head. Andy stepped back again.

"Where do you want Andy?" Kristen asked, "Head or gut?"

Andy didn't answer. He backed up another step. Because of the current situation he was in, Andy didn't notice the rogue book that had slid across the room during Kathleen's accident until he had already stepped on it. His foot slipped. The slip of his foot was miniscule but, with the monitor held over his head, his center of gravity was off. He stumbled backwards, his feet quickly attempting to catch up with the top half of his body, towards the window.

The back of his head connected with the window and the glass pane spiderwebbed out in a hundred directions. Before he had a chance to breathe a sigh of relief, the monitor followed suit and, when it connected with the glass, the window shattered. Andy released the monitor from his grasp, managing to regain his balance as it continued on through the window, toppling from above his head towards the street three stories below.

"Holy..." Was all he could muster, thinking that how close he had almost come to death, when the monitor's cord whipped towards him as it followed the monitor out the window. The cord wrapped itself around his neck like a bolo, and the plug whip-cracked into his eye. He didn't even have a chance to think about his eyeball bursting like a water balloon in his eye socket before the monitor cord was pulled taught around his neck by the rapidly falling monitor. Andy was yanked backwards through the broken window, unable to breath or see with what remained of his right eye. He felt the tension around his neck loosen as the monitor landed with a thud. With his left eye, he caught a glimpse of where the computer monitor had landed, perched precariously on the edge of the closed dumpster. A split second later he felt the asphalt in front of the dumpster slam into his back, he felt one of his lungs burst. His mind raced as he lay on the ground staring past the now broken window of the third-floor apartment and into the black sky beyond.

"I... survived... the... fall," he managed to breathe, a smile forming across his bloodied lips. He breathed a sharp sigh of joy just as the monitor fell forward off of the dumpster and crushed his head.

Another One Bites the Dust

When the water hit his fully clothed body, Josh was not expecting it. He yelped and tried to jump backward but couldn't as his feet were stuck beneath the corpse in the tub. He tumbled forward, groping at the wall in a blind search for the faucet. His hand struck the meaty chest of the body. He reached out as far as he could, but instead of finding the faucet knob, his hand slipped on the wet t-shirt covering the dead body and he pitched forward, falling sideways, and found himself laying side by side with Dave, completely tangled up with the partially amputated dead body. He gave up his search for the faucet and turned his attention instead to freeing himself from the clinging corpse. Unfortunately, the body was slippery and every time he pushed the body off of him, it managed to inch closer and closer.

While attempting to escape from the corpse, Josh's skin began to adjust to the water temperature. He turned his face upwards, towards the spray to rinse the blood from his face. With the blood gone, he was able see again and managed to find a toehold and win his fight for freedom from Dave. He stood up, attempting to kick the body once for good measure, but when he stumbled, he opted for a light nudge as he turned off the water and stepped out of the bathtub, looking around for a towel. When he couldn't find one, he shrugged.

"I guess Kristen isn't just an idiot," He said. He walked out of the bathroom, trying to rub the water from his eyes. As he entered the living room, a cool breeze hit his damp body. He pulled his hands from his eyes and saw Kristen looking out the broken window beside his desk. His eyes went wide. He looked around the room in horror. Paper blowing everywhere, books strewn about, half empty bottles and cans all over the floor, and, on top of everything else, there were more bodies strewn about.

"What the hell happened in when I was in there?" Josh shrieked, his hands running through his wet hair and pulling. Kristen turned and calmly looked at him.

"It's a long story," She said, taking a step towards him, "But I think we should get the hell out of here before the cops show up. I'll tell you on the way." She motioned for the door.

"Whoa…Wait a god damned second," Josh ordered shrilly, "We're just gonna run off together, leaving my apartment filled with…" The words were lost in an incoherent grunt and Josh angrily motioned around the room. Kristen glanced around the room.

"With what?"

"Four bodies, plus another half of a body in my bathtub?" Josh said. Kristen moved towards Josh and took him by the hand.

"That's right," She said, moving in close to him, "And do you know why?"

"No". Josh said, his eyes flitting wildly about as he concentrated on the room surrounding him. Kristen put her fingers under his chin and his eyes stopped moving as they met hers.

"Because this is our chance for us to be together."

"What the hell are you talking about?"

"I've wanted you from day one," Kristen said, "But you never knew when to take a chance. You and I can be together now. Just me and you."

Josh's jaw dropped. Kristen moved her head in, bringing her lips towards his. She kissed him. Josh's mind, suddenly overloaded by thought, couldn't stay on one thing. His mind raced from the corpses, to the option of being a fugitive, to the kiss, to the blood on the walls, to the cold wet clothes he was wearing, and then it returned back to the corpses. It was a sharp pop that pulled Josh out of the whirlpool of thought he was in. Kristen pulled away from the kiss and Josh felt his knees go weak. He wobbled slightly.

"That was one helluva kiss," he muttered to say, his words coming out choppy, slurred and broken. He felt drunk again. He stumbled sideways, his elbow landing on top of the kitchen counter. He held himself there for a moment, trying to stay upright. Then his legs gave out and his arm slid from the counter as he dropped to his knees. He could smell smoke. He looked up at Kristen who still standing in the same spot looking down at him. The pistol was gripped loosely in her right hand, a thin tendril of smoke creeping upwards away from the barrel. Josh cocked his eyebrows and looked at her.

He opened his mouth to ask her what the hell had happened and, though his lips moved, no sound came out. He cleared his throat, coughed, and saw a spray of blood. He sluggishly moved his hand to his mouth, wiping away the blood from his lips. Then he lowered his hands to his belly. It felt wet and tacky. He raised his hands to his eye level and stared at the crimson mess on his fingers. He sank backwards, his ass hitting the floor as his arms fell to his sides, his hands coming to rest on the blood-stained carpet. He raised his head to look at Kristen. He tried to focus, though he felt like a lazy bobblehead doll. Kristen stared back at him, showing no emotion.

"You fucking shot me," he mouthed, a blood bubble forming on his lips. He took a short, shallow breath before he his eyes rolled up into his head and he slumped sideways, collapsing to the ground. Kristen shook her head and sighed. She stepped over Josh's body, moving to the kitchen, then straddled Colleen's lifeless body and began patting her hands along Colleen's pants. After a moment of searching, she hooked her fingers into Colleen's pants pocket and pulled out a set of car keys.

"I'm assuming that you parked the closest," She said to the unconscious form. Colleen didn't respond. Kristen patted her on the stomach before straightening up. Again, she stepped over Josh's body and strode to the door. She opened it, walked out into the hallway, and, without even a cursory glance around the room, she closed the door behind her.

Kristen's Mistake

As Kristen exited the apartment building onto the street, she took in a deep breath of cool fresh air. The sky was no longer an inky black but rather a dusty gray. Dawn would be breaking soon and she knew that she needed to get a move on. Colleen's car was parked right in front of the building and she slid behind the steering wheel. She started the car and began reversing out of the spot. She glanced in the rearview as she was backing up, knowing full well that the street would be deserted at this time of day, but falling victim to habit anyway. When she did, she noticed that she had a streak of blood across her cheek. She brought her hand up to wipe away the blood and saw that the side of her hand also had blood on it. Without stopping the car, she looked down at her hand as she wiped it on the front of her jacket.

There was a jarring thud and Colleen's car lurched to a stop. Kristen's head slammed backwards into the headrest. A horn was blaring from behind her and it took Kristen a moment to realize she was no longer backing up.

"What the fuck?" She said, throwing open the door and stepping out of the car to see that she had backed into someone. She gritted her teeth and raked her fingers through her hair as the other driver stepped out and into the streetlight.

"Hi, Kristen!" Came a voice that was way too chipper to have just been in a collision.

"Brooke?" Kristen asked. Brooke started walking around the car towards Kristen. Kristen opened her mouth but her words were cut off.

"Everyone okay?"

Kristen wheeled around to see the woman from the coffee shop on the first floor of the apartment complex walking towards them. She gave a little wave and motioned towards the two cars.

"That's not a fun way to start the morning," She said, "I called the cops when I saw the accident. What happened?"

Kristen could hear sirens in the distance, moving closer. She realized she had to get the hell out of there before the cops showed up and she knew that she couldn't leave any witnesses. She pulled the gun from her waistband. The store clerk didn't even have time to register what was going on before Kristen pulled the trigger and shot her in the chest. Turning on her heels, Kristen saw Brooke's eyes go wide. She raised the gun and fired again, hitting Brooke in the face. She watched in horror as Brooke's body snapped backwards, her arms flying out to her sides, and her car keys sailed off in the air. They landed on the street, bounced once, and then slid into the opening of the sewer grate on the curb.

The police sirens were even closer now. Kristen thought about running but she knew she wouldn't get very far on foot.

Without a second's further hesitation, Kristen bolted back to the apartment building's front door. Josh, Dan, Andy, and Kathleen all had cars. She figured her best option would be to grab a set of keys off one of them. She yanked open the front door, just as the red and blue lights flared up behind her. She tore up the three flights of stairs to Josh's apartment. As she threw open the door, she decided that it may be best to hole up and wait out the accident scene out front. She slammed the door behind her.

"I need a plan," she said to herself, "And a drink." She crossed the apartment to the kitchen and grabbed the un-opened bottle of Vodka. She took a long pull and angrily threw the bottle across the room. The bottle arced, pouring Vodka over the apartment as it went, before it shattered against the wall, the contents spraying over the room. Kristen lowered her head to her hands.

"Kristen?"

Kristen jerked her head up and spun towards the voice. She took a step backwards and her foot slipped in the puddle of vodka. She lurched backwards, her other foot stepping forward as she tried to regain her balance. It was too late and she lost her footing completely. As her feet flew out from under her, her head met the corner of the open cabinet door and she fell, the side of her face slamming into the corner of the counter. In a spray of blood, she bounced to the floor, landing on top of Colleen's legs.

Colleen rubbed her eyes and shook her head. She had woken up when Kristen threw the bottle across the room but she was still groggy and she could not recall how she had wound up on the floor in Josh's kitchen. She groaned, squinting her eyes against the apartment lights. Her head was throbbing and the room was spinning around her like a carousel. She remembered that she had been drinking and realized she was still drunk. She reached in her pocket and pulled out a cigarette, placing it between her lips. From her other pocket she produced a lighter and she brought the lighter to the cigarette and took a long drag.

"I gotta stop drinking so much," she muttered. She closed her eyes and fell back into unconsciousness. After a moment, the cigarette that had been resting between her lips dropped and landed on her stomach. It rolled from her stomach and onto the floor.

When the burning cigarette landed on the alcohol covered floor, it went up in flames. The fire licked around the kitchen, across the apartment, following the trail of vodka that had been spilled. When the books and papers caught fire the entire apartment was ablaze in a matter of seconds. The smoke alarms sounded, ringing out in the night and signaling the beginning of the end of all of the chaos.

It would be a long time before there was silence once again.